SEALED WITH A KISS

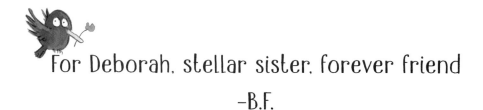

For Deborah, stellar sister, forever friend
—B.F.

Sealed with a Kiss

Text copyright © 2019 by Beth Ferry

Illustrations copyright © 2019 by Olivier Tallec

All rights reserved. Manufactured in China.

Library of Congress Control Number: 2017943581
ISBN 978-0-06-247577-0

The artist used acrylic, pencils, and charcoal to create the illustrations for this book.
Typography by Chelsea C. Donaldson
18 19 20 21 22 SCP 10 9 8 7 6 5 4 3 2 1
❖
First Edition

SEALED WITH A KISS

by BETH FERRY   illustrated by OLIVIER TALLEC

HARPER
An Imprint of HarperCollinsPublishers

Seal was new to the national zoo,
just in from a small zoo in France.
"*Allo*, zoo," she called happily. "Oh, my *chéries*,
what friends we will be."
She waited and waited to be welcomed.
But no one came to meet her, to greet her,
to shower her with kisses.

Then one morning a small sparrow swooped by
and gave Seal a perky peck on the cheek.
Seal was tickled pink.

"Zat is more like it," she said. "I must stop zee waiting
and start participating."
With a smile on her face and a very smelly sardine
in her mouth, Seal ventured forth.

She waddled right up to
Rhino, who sniffed, and
snorted, and sneezed.
"Pee-yew!"

She smooched Panda.
"Ewww!"

She bussed the baboons. **"Blech! Blech! Fish breath!"**

Seal merrily continued on.
She kissed Kangaroo,

cuddled Kookaburra,
canoodled Caribou.

"We've been slobbered!" Kangaroo cried.
"Contaminated," Kookaburra said.
"With squishy, fishy kissies," Caribou added.

The besmooched creatures bemoaned their fate,
scrubbed their faces,
scoured away the kisses . . . and the fishy smell.
"I've been smackereled!" Giraffe cried.
"I've been cod-dled!" Koala moaned.

Seal was oblivious to the collection of groaning, grumbling, gagging animals she left in her wake.

"Zis is the way. I make zee many friends."
She smiled. "*Oui. Oui.*"

Then she kissed Snow Leopard.

Snow Leopard didn't groan or grumble.
He didn't gag. Instead, he growled,

"You stink!"

Seal turned and saw the moaning menagerie behind her.
"Everyone zinks I do not smell like zee rose," she realized.
"Zey zink I stink!"
She blushed scarlet,
turned a sickly shade of green,
and was left feeling nothing but blue.

Sparrow flew in a fluster toward the animals.
"This is no way to treat a new friend," she said.
"Don't you remember when you were new?"

"I do," whispered Koala.
"Me too," said Giraffe.
"She's right," said Rhino.
"We're buffoons," said the baboons.

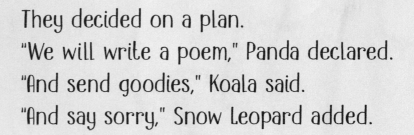

They decided on a plan.

"We will write a poem," Panda declared.

"And send goodies," Koala said.

"And say sorry," Snow Leopard added.

They left their gift by the water's edge.

Seal slowly surfaced.
She read:

DEAR FRIEND,
WE SEALED THIS WITH A LICK
'CAUSE OUR KISSES WOULDN'T STICK,
AND OURSELVES WE WANT TO KICK
'CAUSE WE'RE REALLY ALL HEARTSICK.
WE HOPE THIS DOES THE TRICK.
PLEASE FORGIVE US PRETTY QUICK.
SIGNED,
YOUR NEW ZOO FRIENDS

Seal sighed and sniffed,
then blubbered . . . with happiness.

"Zee rhyme is sublime! And I cannot resist
zee peppermint shrimp!"

As Seal gobbled up the shrimp,
her heavy heart lightened.

She knew exactly how she would say thank you.

With a smile on her face and a
peppermint shrimp in her mouth,
Seal blew kisses to all the animals,

who blew right past Sparrow,
right past the gates, and directly into . . .

Seal's pool.

They covered her with kisses, pecks,
smooches, and smackaroos.
"Now, zat is more like it!" she said.
Because some things,
some special things,
like forgiveness and friendship,
must be sealed with a kiss.

And served with a side of shrimp!

"Oui! Oui!"